Warner Bros.

QUEST FOR CAMELOT™

THE BATTLE FOR CAMELOT

Adapted by Nancy E. Krulik

WORLDWIDE PUBLISHING
TM

SCHOLASTIC INC.

New York   Toronto   London   Auckland   Sydney

ISBN 0-590-12059-X

12 11 10 9 8 7 6 5 4 3 2 1   8 9/9 0 1 2 3/0

Book design by Alfred Giuliani

Printed in the U.S.A.

First Scholastic printing, May 1998

n England, one thousand years ago, the people were divided; fighting hand to hand.

The single hope for peace was in the legend of the sword Excalibur. It was said that only the true king could pull the sword from the stone and unite the people.

Many men had tried. All had failed.

And then a young man stepped forth. His name was Arthur. Arthur easily pulled the sword from the stone and became the rightful king of England.

Within ten years, Arthur and his Knights of the Round Table had built the greatest kingdom on Earth. They called it Camelot. At the end of those ten years, Arthur decreed that he would divide the lands surrounding Camelot equally among all its citizens. This pleased everyone.

Well, almost everyone.

It did not please Sir Ruber. He wanted all the land for himself.

"It is time for a new king . . . and I vote for me!" Ruber told the other Knights of the Round Table.

But the knights could not serve a false king. As Ruber leaped to steal Excalibur from King Arthur, the knights rose up to protect their king and his sword.

During the battle, Ruber killed a knight, Sir Lionel. It was a murder the evil man would live to regret.

The Knights of the Round Table defeated Ruber that day. But Ruber was not one to give up. It took him ten more years, but he finally came up with a successful plan to steal Excalibur. Actually, Ruber didn't do the stealing. Instead, he ordered his Griffin, a magnificent beast with the head and wings of an eagle and the body of a lion, to seize Excalibur for him.

And the word went out across the land: *Excalibur has been stolen!*

Without Excalibur, King Arthur's power was diminished, especially since Arthur had been badly hurt trying to protect his sword from the Griffin. His wizard Merlin could do nothing but urge him to trust in the courage of his people.

Still, Ruber knew that he could not just walk into the castle and declare himself king. He couldn't even go *near* the castle because the Knights of the Round Table were looking for him.

Ruber would have to find someone to help him get inside the castle walls. And he knew just the person.

Lady Juliana, Sir Lionel's widow, was always welcome at King Arthur's court. So Ruber paid Lady Juliana a not-so-friendly visit.

"What do you want?" Lady Juliana demanded of him.

"Camelot!" Ruber replied. "And, pretty Juliana, you're going to help me."

"I refuse!" Lady Juliana declared.

But Ruber made Lady Juliana an offer she could not refuse. His henchmen had already taken her daughter, Kayley, prisoner. "Follow my plan and she won't be hurt," Ruber ordered. Then, using a magic potion, he created a mechanical army of living weapons from his henchmen.

"To the wagons!" Ruber commanded his henchmen. The evil monsters dragged Lady Juliana to a wagon and hitched up the horses. They didn't notice that Kayley had wriggled free! Then they awaited their master's next order.

But the order would not come until Ruber had Excalibur in hand.

Immediately Ruber summoned his Griffin. The mighty beast flew to Ruber's side.

"Panic sweeps across the land," Ruber told the Griffin. "Without the sword, Arthur is vulnerable." The Griffin nodded in agreement.

"And now, Excalibur is mine," Ruber declared.

The Griffin gulped. "Here's where we enter a gray area," he murmured.

Ruber's face grew red with rage. "Excuse me?" he growled. "You lost Excalibur?!"

"I was attacked by a falcon." The Griffin defended himself with a choked voice.

"*What?* My magnificent beast outmatched by a puny little pigeon?" Ruber bellowed.

"It wasn't a pigeon," the Griffin explained. "It was a falcon . . . with silver wings. In a place of untold danger . . . ."

"The Forbidden Forest!" Ruber said. He looked angrily at the Griffin. "How totally stupid you are! Excalibur is the one thing that can keep me from my conquest of Camelot!"

Ruber ordered the beast to return to the Forbidden Forest. The Griffin was scared. The Forbidden Forest was not a nice place to visit. It was full of horrible flesh-eating plants, hungry mud monsters, and fire-breathing dragons.

The Griffin looked at Ruber's angry face. The Griffin had to make a decision: refuse a furious Ruber or return to the Forbidden Forest. The Griffin decided to take his chances with the monsters and dragons!

And Ruber decided he would join him. He did not want to risk losing Excalibur again.

Kayley had overheard Ruber's conversation. Now she was the only person other than Ruber who knew where Excalibur had fallen.

Kayley's father, Sir Lionel, had sworn to protect Excalibur. In his absence, Kayley would do the same. She set off on the road to the Forbidden Forest.

As Kayley discovered, the rumors were all true—the Forbidden Forest was full of treacherous, hidden dangers. But there was also someone very nice in the forest. His name was Garrett. Garrett had once been a stable boy at Camelot. But he'd been blinded and had gone off to live as a hermit in the woods.

Garrett was accompanied by a falcon named Ayden. Ayden protected Garrett by chirping a warning if the young warrior was in danger. Ayden was also a help to Kayley, for he was the silver-winged falcon that had forced Excalibur out of the Griffin's grasp. Ayden could lead Kayley and Garrett to Excalibur.

Before long, Kayley realized that Ruber, the Griffin, and the minions were secretly following them, in the hopes that they would reach Excalibur first. But at each and every turn, Kayley and Garrett managed to outsmart them.

Kayley and Garrett reached Excalibur only minutes before Ruber and his gang. As they left the Forbidden Forest with Excalibur in hand, Ruber and the Griffin were trapped beneath an avalanche of heavy boulders.

It seemed as though King Arthur would get Excalibur back safe and sound.

But anyone who was familiar with Ruber knew that being buried under a couple of heavy boulders couldn't stop him. He still had a few tricks up his sleeve! Ruber ordered his minions to his side. Instantly the evil monsters arrived and began removing the stones from on top of their master. As soon as Ruber was free, he hopped on the Griffin's back and they set off in hot pursuit of Kayley.

Garrett did not go with Kayley to deliver the sword to King Arthur. He had taught Kayley to face her fears, but he had not faced his own. Garrett feared that Kayley would not accept him in Camelot, as she had in the Forbidden Forest. There, he was master of his domain. In Camelot, he would be just a squire . . . a blind squire.

So Kayley was on her way to Camelot alone. She was determined to get Excalibur back in King Arthur's hands by morning.

Ruber had a different fate in mind for the sword.

"I'll take that!" Ruber shouted as he sprang out from behind a bush. He grabbed Excalibur from Kayley's hands.

"Excalibur . . . mine forever!" Ruber said lovingly as he held the sword tight. "You've been quite annoying for a girl," he told the frightened Kayley.

Kayley looked just past Ruber. There she saw her mother's wagon parked behind a tree. Two of Ruber's evil gang, Bladebeak and Spike Slinger, guarded the wagon.

Spike Slinger raced over and grabbed Kayley. They watched as Ruber removed a vial from his pocket and placed the last drop of a powerful magic potion on his palm. His hand began to fizz. The air became filled with green smoke. Suddenly Ruber's arm began to spin so fast it was a blur.

When the motion stopped, Excalibur was permanently fused to Ruber's arm!

"NO!" Kayley cried out in horror.

"Don't worry, little girl," Ruber assured her deviously. "I'll make sure Arthur gets this back. Or *in* the back, as the case may be!"

The henchmen threw Kayley into the wagon. Now both mother and daughter were prisoners. Tearfully, the two embraced.

"What a touching reunion," Ruber snarled. "But all this love is making me nauseous, and you've got a job to do, Juliana. Remember, if you don't . . ."

Lady Juliana watched in terror as one of the minions pointed a spear at her daughter.

"I'll do my job on her!" he announced.

The wagon moved along until it came to the gates surrounding the castle of Camelot. As they neared the drawbridge Ruber hid, warning Juliana, "Not a word. Let's all keep our heads, shall we?"

Lady Juliana looked back at her captive daughter. The spear was still poised against Kayley's neck.

The guard at the castle drawbridge smiled as Lady Juliana approached. He passed word to the castle. Before long a page returned with a message. The King would receive Lady Juliana at the Round Table.

The wagon entered the grounds. It hit a slight bump as it crossed the bridge. Hatchetfoot—the creature who was guarding Kayley—lost his balance and dropped his spear. Kayley kicked him to the floor of the wagon and broke free.

The wagon continued rolling toward the castle keep. The guards were puzzled. They could not understand why the wagon did not stop.

Suddenly Kayley leaped from the back of the wagon. "It's a trick!" she alerted the guards.

But before the guards could order the wagon to halt, Ruber gave an order of his own. "Attack! Seal off the castle!" he commanded his monstrous army.

The guards gave chase, but they were almost powerless against Ruber's deadly army. As the battle continued, Kayley sprang toward the battlements. Ruber's Griffin soared after her. Suddenly Garrett and Ayden appeared at Kayley's side. Word had gotten to Garrett that Kayley had been captured. He'd rushed to her aid as quickly as he could.

Ruber's Griffin spied Ayden. The Griffin was still angry about the battle in which he'd lost Excalibur. The giant beast charged after the falcon, leaving Kayley free to rush to the castle keep. She had to warn King Arthur.

But Ruber was faster than Kayley. He was already inside the building. And his minions had sealed off all the entrances.

Ruber snuck into the Round Table room and pounced upon his prey. "Ta da!" he cried out, surprising King Arthur.

King Arthur lunged and grabbed a spear from the wall. Ruber burst into sinister laughter.

"A spear? How Stone Age," the evil knight taunted King Arthur. "A king would have a more noble weapon." Ruber raised his arm in triumph, revealing Excalibur.

"I'm going to have more fun getting rid of you than when I got rid of Sir Lionel," Ruber declared.

Ruber believed this was a private conversation between Arthur and himself. But Ruber was wrong. He and the king were not the only ones in the castle.

Garrett had led Kayley into the castle through a secret passageway he'd discovered when he was a stable boy. It led to a grate in the floor of the Round Table room.

There, Kayley could hear everything Ruber said. And learning that Ruber had killed her father made Kayley very angry.

Ruber forced King Arthur onto the Round Table.

"I may not survive, but you'll never destroy the ideals of Camelot," King Arthur told Ruber.

"Well, I've got to start somewhere," Ruber snarled. "Say hello to your new king!"

"You are no king," King Arthur said.

"You're right," Ruber agreed. "Perhaps I am more of a god!" Ruber brought Excalibur dangerously close to King Arthur's neck, and gleefully poised himself to deliver the deadly blow.

"I will not serve a false king!" Kayley's voice bellowed from above. She leaped onto a beam and swung through the air. Suddenly, the beam gave way! Kayley landed with a crash right on Ruber's chest. The force sent him soaring through a glass window. Kayley followed close behind.

They landed near the stone that had once held Excalibur. It was then that Kayley remembered that only the true king could pull the sword from that stone.

Slowly, Kayley moved toward the stone.

Ruber followed her. He swung Excalibur hard, but Kayley avoided his blow. Garrett leaped up and attacked Ruber from behind. But Ruber was quick. He grabbed Garrett by the hair and backed him up against the magical stone.

Ruber held Excalibur straight in the air. "Two for the price of one. This must be my lucky day," he shouted as he lunged at Kayley and Garrett.

Just as the sword was about to pierce her and Garrett, Kayley shouted a signal. The two of them dove out of the way. Ruber missed them both and plunged sword-first into the stone!

Ruber tried desperately to pull the sword from the stone. But of course he could not. Ruber could not free himself from the sword, either. It was fused to his arm. Suddenly electric charges crept up from the stone and shot straight up Ruber's arm, destroying his evil forever. Within seconds, Ruber vanished in a burst of light.

An injured King Arthur slowly made his way to the stone. He grasped Excalibur by the handle and gently pulled it free. Once again, Camelot was safe, thanks to the bravery of a young girl and a blind warrior.

Kayley and Garrett were justly rewarded for their good deed. "You have reminded us that a kingdom's strength is not based on the strength of the king, but on the strength of the people," the king told Kayley and Garrett.

Good King Arthur then used Excalibur for a most noble cause. He tapped the brave duo on the shoulders, and dubbed them Knights of the Round Table.